43 Bin Street

Livi Michael

ORCHARD BOOKS

To Paul and Ben,
with love

CONTENTS

Chapter One
We're going to die!

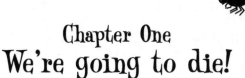

"Now what are we going to do?" quavered Nattie, as a freak draught from nowhere at all slammed the door shut behind us.

I joined her on the ceiling, landing with a semi-roll, and extending my legs so that the pads on my feet stuck.

"Er," I said, decisively.

We had already explored the windows, which were sealed tight. I thought hard, which isn't easy when you're upside down.

"Well," – I said eventually, and Nattie looked at me hopefully. "Don't know," I said, and in each of the panels of her compound eyes, I could see the hope dwindling.

I groomed the sticky hairs on my legs, which is something I do when I'm pretending I'm not worried. "What do you think?" I asked.

Nattie rose a little, hovered, then flitted backwards and forwards, which is something she does when she's not pretending.

"We're going to die!" she said, flapping her wings forwards and back.

Nattie's not an optimist like me, but she did have a point. There in the topmost corner of the room, spinning the biggest web we'd ever seen, was an enormous spider.

To get the full effect you have to imagine a spider twenty times bigger than you, with eight eyes each twice as big as you, and eight enormous hairy legs. Each of the hairs on its legs is nearly as big as you, and from its bulging abdomen it's spinning a web, one of several that are rapidly covering the ceiling. A thread shoots out like a super-long, super-sticky rope, a rope covered in the stickiest, fly catching glue in the world, and the spider bounds along it, coming a foot nearer to us each time.

"*Do* something!" Nattie buzzed.

I sucked thoughtfully through my proboscis.

"I'm thinking," I said.

The irony is, we only came up here to get away from the woodlice, who were driving us crazy with their munching song.

Munch-munch, munch-munch, munch, munch, munch.

All day long they're at it. *Munch-munch-munch-munch-munch.* Ever since the Hodge family moved out we've been living in an empty house that has gradually been invaded by moths and midges, beetles and silverfish. None of whom has much in the way of conversation.

Have you ever tried having a conversation with a silverfish?

"Plug, plug, plug, plug, plug, plug, plug." That's all *they* say. Or occasionally, when more of them come swarming up into the sink. "*Plughole!*" looking really pleased with themselves. But it's hardly a talking point, is it?

The spider was now so close that we could see ourselves reflected a hundred times in each of the multiple panels of its eight eyes. We could see digestive juices dripping from its mandibles.

"Kiko," Nattie said. "Think faster."

My name's Kiko, by the way. Kalvin Irving Kerry Oswald 492, but you can call me Kiko. Female flies lay more than 2000 eggs, and have run out of names. So each fly has a name and a number; Kiko 492, Nattie 235. That way we don't get mixed up. Killed and eaten, yes; mixed up, no.

Nattie rose into the air again, her

feelers quivering and her hum rising in pitch. She'd just noticed what I spotted right away. There were two more spiders in the room, bounding towards us on their sticky ropes.

Flies don't like other insects much. But we *hate* spiders.

I filled my thorax with air.

"OK Nattie," I hummed, trying to sound as though I had a plan. "We're going to have to make a dash for it."

This wasn't as easy as it sounds. Imagine that all you can see before you is a mass of sticky rope, criss-crossed this way and that, all over the walls and ceiling. In the time it took for Nattie to say "Dash for what?" more tangled strands shot out towards our corner of the ceiling.

This was going to be a challenge.

"Follow me, Nattie!" I cried, breathing in enough air to fill both thorax and abdomen, and spreading both pairs of wings. "Do exactly what I do!"

With a single bound I was airborne. As a thread shot towards me I dived to avoid it and narrowly missed a tangled knot of threads from the other spider. I shot upwards again and grazed my wings on a sticky line. If only we could get away from the mass of web!

This was going to take more flying skill than your average fly ever learns. Luckily I graduated first from my flying class. Even in my sleep I could navigate through cross currents of air, and now I was very much awake. I searched the annals of fly memory for every trick we've ever learned in the course of our evolution. The loop, the dive, the slow roll, the point roll, the inverted spin, the bunt and the pinwheel…

I didn't dare look behind me, but fortunately, with my 360 degree vision I could tell Nattie was keeping up. Struggling, but keeping up. Her eyes looked huge and terrified. But then, her eyes always look huge and terrified. Lower and lower we flew, looking for a loophole in the tangled mass of threads.

And at last I saw it, way below, and hardly bigger than a fly. This was going to take all my diving skill.

"Follow me, Nattie!" I cried.

A single wing tip, moved the tiniest fraction, gives a smooth, sweeping curve at tremendous speed. A fraction too much and you're into a headlong spin, but there was no time to worry about that now. Speed is power, speed is joy. Speed will also kill you, of course, but it's a mistake to think too hard about that. I levered my wings back and plummeted so hard that all the air I'd stored was driven out of my body and whistled past my hearing valves in a high pitched hum.

And did it! Straight through the hole with pinpoint accuracy, out into free air. I sucked it in, filling my body once more, and with the same high-pitched drone Nattie shot down beside me.

"Fly low Nattie!" I cried. I don't know why, but flying low takes up less energy. You can hold your wings out still and glide along, swerving at the last minute towards the keyhole. The biggest spider swung after us, *splat*! into the wood but we were out in the corridor.

"We made it!" panted Nattie.

Chapter Two
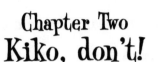

But now where to go? All the downstairs rooms were sealed off, windows and front door locked, which was how we'd got trapped in there in the first place with all the beetles and moths.

As I said, flies don't like other insects. We like humans. We have a name, a number and a household. When I emerged from my larval state, my mum said, "Right, Kiko, you take number 43 with Nattie. Grandad's in number 45. I'll be in number 53 if you need anything."

"But what do I do?" I asked, whirring my newly-formed wings.

"Help the humans recycle their food," she said, "And keep them well-exercised. You'll work it out."

And we did. It was a doddle. Number 43 Bin Street was full of slow, lumbering humans who ate a lot. Perfect. We had them running from room to room, batting their arms about and shouting, till they all looked quite muscular and fit. They never *caught* us, of course. House flies beat their wings 330 times a second, and stay permanently airborne. We have tiny hairs all over our bodies, just like you do, but we pay attention to ours. We can detect changes in air flow and react five times faster than you do. Some of the hairs are sticky, so that we can walk up glass and onto ceilings. We have compound eyes, with 360 degree vision. So we see the full picture. Unlike you lot, who can't even see where you're going.

But you don't give up, I'll say that much. Flies respect that. Because we don't give up either. That's part of the Mission each fly learns as a maggot.

If you want to be a fly, fly, fly,

You have to try, try, try.

Anyway, there we were, me and Nattie, exercising our humans and living off the lovely clumps and splashes and trickles and spatters and crumbs they trailed behind them, when one day, everything changed.

First there was all this rumpus and upheaval. Furniture moving, boxes being packed, humans lumbering about and swearing, dishes smashed, people falling over things. Everything was packed, stacked or rolled up into a huge van. Or two. You humans never did learn the art of travelling light. Sofas, stereos, TVs, double beds – you'd think a whole town was on the move.

Then silence.

Nothing.

All the rooms seemed huge.

We buzzed about a bit feeling lost. No more food except for dried up bits on the kitchen surfaces, a splash of soup on the skirting board and an elderly lump of liver in the meter cupboard. We couldn't live for long on that.

Then before long the other insects started arriving.

Firstly the woodlice, burrowing their way through the floorboards, then the ants, pouring in through cracks and crannies, then the silverfish swarming upwards through the drains into the sinks and bath. Midges flew in through a crack in the window. Cockroaches and earwigs munched their way through the plaster, dustmites burrowed into the one pair of curtains that were left. Tiny green and red beetles crawled along the cracks in the window frames, moths butted themselves against the windows at night, too stupid to understand glass.

But of course the spiders were the worst. Great fat spiders, weaving huge sticky webs that stretched from one corner of the ceiling to the other. And there we were, trapped with all these creepy crawlies, and not a human in sight.

A fly without a human is like a bee without pollen, it says in the Flyrule. And how right that was. No point to our existence. Nothing to do. We might die here in an empty house, alone.

Well, not if I could help it. A fly is the most resourceful creature on earth, every maggot knows that. And hadn't Grandad told us the story, many times, of how Menelaus, King of Sparta invoked the goddess Athena for strength against his enemy, Hector, and she gave him the courage of a fly?

'Grandad,' I thought sadly, as we

buzzed along the empty corridor, 'where are you now?'

"He's next door," said Nattie. "Where he's always been."

A fly has no private thoughts. They all sort of leak out in his buzz.

How to get next door, though, that was the thing. The doors to the bedrooms were shut, and it was no use flying in through the keyholes, because the windows were jammed shut too.

The door to the bathroom was open however. The bathroom window was shut like all the others, but there was the sink.

If a creature like a silverfish, that has no visible signs of intelligence, can use a plughole…

"Kiko," said Nattie, sternly, "Don't!"

But I had already flown in and paused, hovering, over the sink.

Flies don't like plugholes. There's the risk of getting your wings wet, and the fact that spiders use plugholes as well as silverfish, so you never know what you might meet. On the other hand, I was sick of being shut up in a house with no humans and hardly any food. The taps hadn't been turned on for weeks – it should be fairly dry...

"I'm going in," I said to Nattie.

"Oh no Kiko," Nattie moaned. But I was already in my fast dive, hurtling towards the metallic hole.

And in I bombed. Straight into some startled silverfish who were pouring themselves upwards, chanting the usual *"Plug-plug-plug-plug, plug-plug-*

plgurkk...!" as I landed scattering them all into a flat spin.

"Out of my way!" I hummed, charging through them all, buzzing like a power drill. I was right about it being dry down there. There was some lovely grungy stuff trapped in the u-bend and a clump of hair as big as a net, but nothing a Superfly can't charge his way through. Then up the curve, round another bend into a narrower pipe, and out through the overflow that led through the wall.

"We're out! We're out!" I sang, breathing in the fresh air that smelled of green living plants and dustbins. "We did it!"

Now might have been the time for Nattie to show some gratitude.

'You did it, Kiko,' she might say, 'You

saved us both, you brave, clever fly!'

Instead of which she shook her wings out sulkily and said, "That was disgusting. And you could have killed us both!"

"Well, I didn't hear you coming up with any ideas!"

"*I* wouldn't have gone upstairs in the first place."

Item 1 in the Flyrule: always work in pairs if possible. Nattie wouldn't have gone upstairs in an empty house – she was following me. But without me she'd never have any adventures!

"I got us out didn't I?" I said, buzzing in the warmth of the sun.

"Let's try to find Grandad," Nattie said, looking round nervously at the birds.

Fortunately this bit was easy. The

kitchen window of number 45 was wide open, and lots of lovely, greasy smells were wafting out. Inside, Grandad's human, Bernie Dibble, was drinking beer from a can. Grandad was having a sip with him, tasting the droplets of beer round the ring-pull through his feet.

"Grandad! Grandad!" we chorused.

Grandad raised his bleary, compound eyes from the top of the can.

"Why, it's…" he began. Then we could see him searching his memory annals. This takes a while. A fly's memory annals go back nearly 400 million years. We keep all our history encoded in our buzz. The longer we buzz, the more of our history unravels itself. And this isn't our actual grandad, who was accidentally stir-fried when he flew into a wok. This is *his* grandad. He has 47 million descendants, which makes it a bit tricky when it comes to names.

You know when you talk to an old person, perhaps your own grandad, and you can see them searching their memories for stories that go back perhaps fifty years? Well, with Grandad you can see him processing information right back from the Devonian era, through the Carboniferous, up through the Permian, the Triassic, the Jurassic, Cretaceous, Palaeocene, Eocene, Oligocene, Miocene, Pliocene and the Pleistocene, very, very slowly arriving at Now. As we watched him trying to remember our names we could see images of the continents fusing and splitting apart, reflected in the panels of his eyes.

But we were starving! Eventually Nattie helped him out.

"Kiko and Nattie," she said.

"Of course you are," said Grandad rising into the air and performing the little bow peculiar to Elders. "Welcome. You remind me of two flies I once knew – Mico and Pattie – or was it Bino and Fattie?"

"Grandad, we're really hungry," Nattie said.

"Of course, of course," mumbled Grandad. "Help yourselves to Bernie."

Without further ado, we landed.

Bernie is a house-fly's dream. He never washes, he never cleans. Plant your sticky legs down on that vest and they come away even stickier than before. Tomato ketchup, sardines, porridge, tomato ketchup on top of porridge – just sink your proboscis in through the layers and suck!

And he isn't just crusted in grime, he kind of leaks. Even his sweat tastes of pizza. There was enough food here to keep a whole swarm happy. Furiously we sucked and puked.

Grandad watched us, beaming.

"It's a cornucopia of culinary delights," he said. Grandad's vocabulary is nearly as long as his memory.

"Yum, gobble slurp," we agreed.

Grandad looked horrified when we told him we'd been trapped in an empty house.

"When there's no humans about,

A fly must move out,"

he said, reprovingly.

Yes, well, we know that now, don't we? But number 43 Bin Street was our first ever household. How were we to know that humans moved?

Grandad settled down on Bernie's can again, shaking his antenna.

"You must stay here with me," he said. And so we did.

We introduced Bernie to the idea of exercise, which was obviously a whole new concept for him. He'd grown used to Grandad, who didn't flap about and buzz too much any more, but he wasn't prepared for two young super-fit and active flies buzzing and humming around his face, cleaning out his ear wax for him, and his nasal hair. Over the next few days we became quite attached to Bernie, mainly because he was so sticky, and because we'd gone for so long without humans to take care of, we were determined to do a thorough job.

"I think that might be enough now, Kiko," Nattie said, hovering just a little way in front of Bernie. "Remember, we have to exercise him until he's pink, not purple."

This is a very important item in the Flyrule.

PINK GOOD, PURPLE BAD.

If a human goes purple, or blue, they're in trouble.

Bernie was perspiring freely and a little out of breath. He sank back in his chair with a moan, allowing me and Nattie to land on his vest, and pluck the scrambled eggs from the hairs on his chest.

But Bernie seemed to have lost his appetite after chasing us away from his food. He pushed his plate away, mopping his forehead. It was clear we were going to have to do a lot of recycling for him.

Ah, Bernie, Bernie! Whatever would you do if we weren't around? You wouldn't get any exercise, and you'd waste whole troughs full of food without recycling. Great clumps of it left to congeal in the bin.

"Whoops – waste alert!" said Nattie.

The trick is to get to the food before it hits the bin and spray as much recycling fluid over the surface as possible. This isn't easy with Bernie's great hams batting the air to drive us off.

Of course I know that Bernie knows he

needs us. We clear up after him, we keep him exercised, but what does he do?

Swats at us with his newspaper.

"It's all part of the game!" Nattie cried rising gaily on the current of air from Bernie's newspaper. Whoosh! And again! "Humans love to play!"

But sometimes he seems really angry. Almost as if he doesn't *want* us to vomit on his toast.

"Sometimes I think Bernie doesn't appreciate us," I said to Grandad that evening after Bernie had gone to bed. Grandad looked very shocked.

"Oh, you mustn't think that," he said. "Humans need flies. They'd be lost without us. Humans and flies belong together. For one thing, we clean up their mess, and they make enough of that. For another, we taught them to fly…"

Nattie and me settled in on the kitchen table, where there were still lots of crumbs left from Bernie's meal, droplets of bacon fat, rings of sugary tea. We could sense a story coming on. Grandad knows a lot of good stories. And they're all very long.

Chapter Three
Imagine wings!

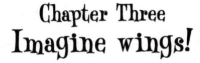

"It all started two million years ago," he began. "Temperatures dropped. England started drifting and tilting about. All sensible beasts migrated to warmer climes. Like Africa…

"…it was there that our ancestress, Noli 94, was laying her eggs on a nice patch of mammoth dung. When she looked up there he was. A man-ape standing up for the first time, looking at the stars.

"'There'll be trouble,' she said. And how right she was. This first ancestor of man was completely blown away by the evening sky. The stars were much bigger and brighter in those days, like a huge, brilliant patchwork full of patterns. He'd never seen anything like it, going around on all fours with his nose pressed to the floor, sniffing out grubs. He just stood and stared. You could practically see his brain evolving as he looked.

"In those days his brain hadn't evolved very far. Barely had early man got it together to point a trembling finger at Orion and say 'Ug!' when *wallop*, up comes the mountain lion and eats him.

"Nothing left of him but a pile of bones, gristle and hair.

"Over the next few thousand years this tragic story was repeated many times. Let's face it – you humans just weren't built to survive. You couldn't fly, you can't see or hear very well, you made more noise than a herd of rhinos. Anything bigger than a wombat or faster than a giant sloth just ate you. The ice ages froze you, and when the air warmed up, viruses multiplied and killed you off. Great dust storms blew you away, the deserts destroyed you. I mean, we were used to watching the great circle of life and death, but this was just pitiful. Another ancestor, Arkon 68, proved conclusively that you don't notice danger. Too busy paddling to notice the crocodiles. Too busy looking up at the stars to notice the mountain lion.

"Finally Coran the Wise shook his proboscis and said, 'We have to help them out. They'll be extinct before they get started.'

"Conferences were held. Great fly-moots, attended by billions of flies. And it was at one of these that our most famous ancestress, Hester 44, came up with her Great Idea.

"'What,' she said, rising and hovering gracefully above the multitude, 'Is our single most important attribute? The gift we can pass on to the human race?'

"Twenty six trillion, seven hundred and eighty five billion, six hundred and forty nine million, four hundred and twenty two thousand, three hundred and eighty six flies rubbed their front legs together and scratched their heads.

"'We can vomit all day long?' ventured one. Hester looked at him.

"'Why would they need to do that?' she asked, not unkindly. 'They can't find enough food as it is.'

"Twenty six trillion, seven hundred and eighty five billion, six hundred and forty nine million, four hundred and twenty two thousand, three hundred and eighty six flies looked stumped. The low droning noise made by a stumped fly swelled to an oceanic roar across the vast African plains. Hester flitted about impatiently in mid-air.

"'We can *fly*,' she said at length, exasperated.

"Well, it seemed obvious when she put it like that. But right across Africa twenty six trillion, seven hundred and eighty five billion, six hundred and forty nine million, four hundred and twenty two thousand, three hundred and eighty six flies formed themselves into a gigantic question mark.

"'We can teach them to *fly*!' said Hester. And gradually the low droning noise changed to an excited buzz. The giant question mark changed to a giant exclamation mark. It was simple. It was brilliant. There was only one problem.

"'How?' asked Arkon 1344, from his position at the very tip of the giant exclamation mark.

"Twenty six trillion, seven hundred and eighty five billion, six hundred and forty nine million, four hundred and twenty two thousand, three hundred and eighty six pairs of compound eyes swivelled towards the low scrub trees, where early man, a solid mass of muscle, bone and hair lumbered about, falling over tree roots, stones, his own feet, and well, anything else really. Crashing to the ground so heavily the whole earth shook.

"It didn't look very likely.

"But Hester 44 was not a fly to be put off by details.

"'First we have to put the idea into his mind,' she said firmly. 'We have to make sure he *notices* us.'

"There was some shuffling and grumbling in the ranks. Mutterings of, 'What mind?' and 'Well, if he doesn't notice the sabre-toothed tiger…' but Hester's voice rose above them all.

"'We are the agents of human destiny,' she said impressively, silencing everyone.

'The race of fly has no more important mission than this. *Stay close* to them. Keep them company at all times. Sooner or later, one of them is bound to catch on.'

"And from that day to this we've followed you around. Out of the open grassy plains and deserts into the woods, from the woods to the caves, from caves to little mounds of mud and straw not unlike beavers or muskrats make, from them to stone huts, from small clusters of stone huts to proper villages and towns, then cities with high-rise buildings and motorways.

"No one could call us impatient.

"One million, nine hundred and ninety seven thousand, five hundred years later another fly-moot was held.

"'They're not catching on,' sighed Arkon 44925.

"Through all those years of human evolution we had buzzed around your faces, up your noses, in your ears. 'Fly, fly, fly,' we'd buzzed. We'd hovered around you beating our wings 330 times a second, showing you how to stay permanently airborne. We'd shown you arabesques, spiralling, nose dives – even how to mate in mid air, but were you interested? One million, nine hundred and ninety seven thousand, five hundred years of being swatted at and chased round room with scrolls of papyrus and even tablets of stone, we were beginning to feel as though we weren't getting anywhere.

"There had been human casualties, of course.

"One particularly persistent agent, Mika 222, had lodged herself in the ear of her human, even laying her eggs in its warm, waxy interior, and had kept up a persistent song.

"'Fly fly fly fly, fly fly fly.'

"He didn't like it at first, and had gone around batting his own head. But gradually he got used to it, and even hummed along. Then one night he woke from a powerful dream of flying over the edge of the world and sat up in his bed.

"'I can fly,' he yelled, frightening his wife to death. And he went out of the door of his hut, along the path to the cliff, spreading his arms out as he ran, faster and faster...

"'Noooooo!' buzzed Mika 222.

"Too late.

"He plummeted over the edge of the cliff.

"Naturally this had shaken everyone up. No fly wants his human to come to any harm. You might swat at us with anything that comes to hand, and even, on very rare occasions, do actual damage, but we know you're only playing. Like big, harmful puppies – you just don't know your own strength.

"So everyone sympathised with Mika, who had exited the ear just in time, over the untimely end of her human.

"'I just feel as though it's all my fault,' she said, and we all clustered round to reassure her.

"'You weren't to know.'

"'No one could have tried harder.'

"'You made him dream about

flying – that's a real breakthrough!'

"'The problem is,' hummed Basil 246, 'That they haven't got any wings.'

"There it was. The thought that had occurred to every fly at some point in his lonely endeavours, spoken aloud for the first time. No wings, no flight.

"Everyone looked glum.

"But finally, another fly of ideas, also called Hester (since that first Hester had shown us the way forward, all flies of ideas had been called Hester) rose up into the air.

"'We have to make them *imagine* wings!' she said. And simultaneously, we all saw the magic of that idea. Get the human imagination to work and you could do anything. Flies everywhere changed their tune.

"'Wings wings wings wings, wings wings wings,' we buzzed.

"And gradually it began to work.

"Images of winged creatures began appearing in the things you made, *and* in your stories! The Greeks came up with Pegasus, a winged horse, King Etena of Babylon was featured on a coin, flying on an eagle's back, King Kaj Kaoos of Persia was said to have attached eagles to his throne and flown around his kingdom, Alexander the great did the same with griffins. At practically the same time there was the legend of Icarus in Greece, and the Peruvian leader, Auca, was said to have wings and could fly.

"And finally, all over the middle east, images of men with wings, called angels, began featuring in stories and paintings.

Yes! Flies everywhere were so excited. And after that, well, comparatively speaking, it was fast work.

"The first real breakthrough came in China, where kites were invented. In no time at all they were strapping young boys to them, and sending them out to test the weather, or to spy on enemy camps. Then for a few centuries, people everywhere tried strapping feathers on wooden frames to their arms and jumping off tall buildings, with messy results.

"Still, 'You can't hatch a maggot without breaking an egg,' as Hester 84379 reminded us all. And eventually, just over a thousand years ago, a monk in England was the first man to fly about 125 human paces, with home-made wings.

"Course, he did break both his legs.

Still, an event worth recording in the fly's memory archive.

"After that, it was downhill for a while. A man in Constantinople made wings like the sails of a boat, plummeted from the top of a tower and died. A man in France made wings that actually flapped using a kind of spring, but he fell to his death when the spring broke.

"'We have to keep the larger picture in mind,' Hester 99264 said.

"Then, about 500 years ago, a man called Leonardo da Vinci invented the first design for a flying machine! The ornithopter.

"None of us had foreseen this, but we all saw the potential. If man couldn't fly himself – too solid, no muscles to speak of – he could invent machines! We all watched Leonardo with great interest. The poor man never understood why his studio was so full of flies. But he turned out to be something of a disappointment. Got caught up in other things.

"'Never mind the Mona Lisa,' his fly, Noli 2486 would tell him regularly. 'Get on with the flying machine!'

"But he never did. It was almost 300 years later that two brothers in France, Joseph Michel and Jacques Etienne Montgolfier came up with...the hot air balloon! They used the smoke from a fire to blow hot air into a silk bag, and the bag rose!

"The balloon was propelled by burning a pile of moist wool and old shoes. The first passengers were a rooster, a duck and a sheep. Don't ask me why. Most of

France seemed to be gathered in the great field watching. Flies gathered from all over Europe. The crowds swatted at us with handkerchiefs and napkins. The balloon rose to 6,000 feet and travelled more than a mile!

"The rooster and the duck seemed to take to this without complaining, but the sheep was terribly confused. Walked round in little circles when it was let out, then just lay down. But the crowd went wild. Celebrations went on for more than a week. Feasting and music. But it was nothing to the excitement felt by flies. We clutched one another in mid air and danced. We got drunk on the free-flowing champagne. At last! At last. Soon people were going up regularly in balloons. And from there on it was just a short step to…

"The glider! In England George Cayley designed a machine that could be controlled by the movements of the body, strapped a small boy that no one knew very well into it, and pushed him off a cliff. It flew! And it flew, and it flew. It took some time to retrieve the small boy, but eventually he was found, safe and well in a prickly bush, surrounded by collapsed glider and a little swarm of flies all buzzing loudly so that people would know where he was.

"Now things were really speeding up. In 1852 the first steam-powered airship was flown by Henri Giffard, and a fly called Luigi. In 1890 Clement Ader flew a steam-powered, bat-winged monoplane for fifty metres near Paris.

And in 1892, the Wright brothers, Orville and Wilbur, opened their first bicycle shop and set about designing bikes with wings.

"The rest, as they say, is history. Air mail, satellite TV, and, something that no fly had ever envisaged – rockets to the moon and the planets…

"…Through thousands of years of trial and error," Grandad said, "Flies were humans' constant companions. They'd never have got this far without our help and encouragement. We followed them everywhere, even to Antartica – now that was a challenge. Whenever some human like Amy Johnson or Amelia Earhart set a new flight record, when William E. Boeing designed his first commercial passenger plane, there was always some fly around, buzzing helpfully inside their helmets. One of our more intrepid agents, Mizi 493, even tried getting into the space rocket to follow Buzz Aldrin to the moon, but she got distracted by the buffet."

Grandad seemed to have finished his long story. There was a silence in which he started to snooze. Suddenly it looked as if he was about to fall into the half cup of cocoa Bernie had left on the kitchen table. Me and Nattie propped him up, and I said, "Well, now they can fly, they don't need us any more, do they?"

Grandad looked shocked all over again.

"You mustn't even think that," he said. "Human beings need us more than ever."

He expanded his wings gently and folded them again, looking suddenly very sad. "The machine has been their lasting burden and sorrow," he said. "The tragedy and destiny of the whole human race."

We looked at him blankly. "Er – why?" I asked.

Grandad's antennae quivered. "Look at the mess they make! All those machines cluttering up the atmosphere, all the fuel, all the wreckage. And what do they use them for?"

A shaft of moonlight glimmered in each panel of his compound eyes.

"War. Their machines make death."

He sighed. "No sooner were planes invented than there was World War I. Every fly in six continents was involved in clearing up and decomposition duties. And once we sorted all that out, what happened? World War II.

No fly saw that coming.

"No, flying has been a disaster for humans. They can't get on with one another like flies. If only they could learn from us how to co-operate with one another. Or to evolve. A bit of evolution goes a long way. But why bother when you've got contraptions doing all the work?"

Grandad shook his proboscis sadly, and tiny drops of cocoa flew out. "Too lazy to evolve, that's man. We evolved. Over thousands of years we became domestic insects, wholly devoted to the welfare of man. They even gave us a different name. *Musca domestica*, that's us. But man can't be bothered evolving, same as he can't be bothered to exercise now that he's got all the machinery carrying him around. Take climbing for instance – all the ropes, pickaxes, rucksacks they carry around with them – when all they need is good sticky hair on their feet. We could teach them a lot about climbing, though it might take another two million years. And recycling – we *invented* that! Where would they be without recycling?

"No," Grandad said. "Humans need flies more than ever now. They wouldn't be *here* if it wasn't for us. Human welfare is our mission. Don't you forget that, er – "

"Kiko," I said helpfully.

"It's been centuries since we had anything to add to the Flyrule about humans," Grandad said, and there was a nostalgic look in his many eyes. "We can teach them anything they need to know – except how to get on together.

That'd be the real challenge," he said. "But there's a long way to go."

And he was off, skating like a champion across the sausage fat in Bernie's pan. We could only watch in admiration as he looped round the sausages on three of his six legs, scooping up bits of egg without getting his feet scorched or the tiniest droplet of fat on his wings. That's our grandad, virtuoso sky-diver, figure skater, and stunt-fly extraordinaire!

Chapter Four

Bernie certainly had a long way to go when it came to tidying up. All the rooms of his house were full of used pots and dishes, cups half full of grimy tea, glasses with the dregs of beer inside. He didn't wash up and he never changed his vest. All that week we were kept busy with recycling and decomposition duties, while he ran after us shouting and batting his arms around.

Then, at the end of the week Nattie called me over to the window.

"Kiko, look!" she called in a state of great excitement.

A van was pulling up outside number 43 Bin Street!

"It's our new family, I know it is," Nattie buzzed, and she clutched me. "Maybe there'll be a baby!"

Babies are good. Lovely greasy blobby things, soaked in their very own recycling fluid, which humans call 'wee'. Nattie and I held on to one another, hovering, as the van doors opened, waiting for the big, noisy happy family to spill out.

But there was only one woman and one small boy.

They were both very pale, and very neat. They were dressed in identical light blue trousers and t-shirts and their pale hair was combed firmly back. They had two boxes, and a large suitcase, that was all. They stood staring, without blinking, not at their own garden, which was untidy enough, since the Hodge family never had got round to mowing the lawn, but at Bernie's.

Bernie's garden was about forty feet long, and looked as though a skip had been overturned in it. There were mattresses, pram wheels and half a shed scattered across it, a rusting washing machine and carburettor. There was a metal frame that had once had a swing on it, a rocking horse, and several doors. There was a supermarket trolley full of bricks, an old toilet, and an inflatable whale. The new people took all this in, tilting their heads first one way then the other. They looked like two very worried chickens.

Sometimes it's hard for us flies to tell you humans apart.

There was only a hedge dividing their part of the garden from Bernie's, and where the hedge was sparse, several planks with nails driven into them had fallen through. Other bits of rubbish had found their way over from his garden to theirs, and already we could see that this would be about as welcome as a cow pat in a picnic. Soon Bernie himself could be heard tugging his way out of his front door, which stuck. He came out into the garden scratching himself, and gave a terrific belch. Then he saw the new neighbours, and his face lit up. He leaned across the hedge in his spattered vest and said, "Hello – who are you?"

The woman turned even paler than before. For a moment I thought that she might scream or faint, but she said, "Mrs Spick," and closed her mouth up primly.

Bernie shook his head and some crisps fell out of his ear. "Bernie Dibble," he said. "You the new neighbours then?"

Mrs Spick took her son's hand firmly. "Come along, Tarquin," she said, heading for the house.

"Mum," said Tarquin, "Can't I play in the garden?"

"Clean first, play later," said Tarquin's mum, and she opened one of the boxes. It was full of every possible kind of cleaning fluid, polish, spray, window leather, dusters, pan scrubs and bleach.

"There's a lot to do," she said.

"Oh, let the lad play," said Bernie. "I'll give you a hand if you like."

Mrs Spick looked at him with thinly veiled horror.

"No thank you, Mr Dribble," she said.

"Dibble," said Bernie. "But you can call me Bernie," he added. He leaned further across the hedge. "And what shall I call you?"

"Mrs Spick," said Tarquin's mum, dragging the first box inside.

The next few hours were a whirr of activity as Tarquin and his mum set about the empty house. There was the roar of the vacuum cleaner and the washing machine, the squeak of a window leather, the whish-whish of dusters and the strong smell of bleach and disinfectant. Nattie and me hovered outside the windows, trying to peer in, and almost getting soaped for our pains. We'd never seen anything like it. The Hodge family had dragged a Hoover round the carpet every two weeks or so; Bernie never did.

"Well, it looks like she's got rid of the spiders," Nattie murmured in a low buzz, as Tarquin carried the twenty-eighth one to the wheelie bin on a clean sheet of paper.

At last there was a pause in the activity. Mrs Spick hung a glossy portrait of a vacuum cleaner over the fireplace, and started to feed Tarquin. Me and Nattie thought this might be a good time to fly in and help with the crumbs. After all, it was our house.

"You first," I said to Nattie.

"No, you."

The truth was, we were a little nervous of our old home. It didn't *smell* like home. But it was dinner time, and Mrs Spick did appear to be cooking. Eventually we flew in through the one small window pane she had left open. The smells of bleach and disinfectant became sickeningly strong, but we braved these in the interests of Grub.

Mrs Spick had her back to Tarquin, so we were able to fly quite close to his plate.

"Whatever is she feeding him?" Nattie buzzed.

On Tarquin's plate there was a small cube, that looked like a cube of washing powder. It didn't look like food, and it didn't smell like food either.

"Rubber gloves on, Tarquin," said Mrs Spick.

What was going on?

I was just about to land on the greenish cube, to investigate further, when Mrs Spick turned round, carrying a small, hand-held Hoover. She gave a huge shriek like a whistling kettle.

"Flies!" she screamed. "Filthy, germ-ridden pests!"

"How rude!" said Nattie, rising gracefully.

"Who are you calling...?" I started to say, but before I could get the words out, Mrs Spick had plucked something metallic from her apron pocket and pressed the nozzle at one end.

Instantly a hissing jet of something toxic sprayed right at us. We fell back choking and unable to see. I spiralled downwards, just remembering to flap my wings in time. Nattie butted into the door frame.

But the woman didn't finish there. She charged round after us, still shrieking and spraying us with toxic waste. We butted blindly into windows and walls.

"All right, all right," I tried to say. "We're going!" But I couldn't get the words out for choking.

At last we found the open door and Nattie tugged me out of it, choking and blinded herself. We spun round the garden a few times feeling very sick and dizzy, before landing on Bernie's old mattress.

"What – was – that?" I gasped.

Nattie didn't know, and could hardly

speak. There seemed to be nothing for it, but to follow Bernie back into his house, where Grandad was just having his afternoon nap.

"Well, hello!" he said, falling off his plate. "I thought you two were going back home."

"We can't," said Nattie.

"The new woman won't let us," I told Grandad. "She doesn't want flies in her house."

Grandad looked astonished. "Not want flies?" he said. "That's nonsense. Every household needs a fly. She'll want you, all right, she just doesn't know how to make you welcome."

I shook my proboscis, which was burning.

"No, grandad, she really doesn't,"

I said, and I told him about the spray.

"Fly-spray?" Grandad said, "But that's terrible." He rose a few feet in the air, in agitation. "When will humans realise that the world wasn't just made for them?" he said and he flapped off into a worried hum about the plight of the human race. Finally he landed again.

"You two had better stay with me," he said.

And so we did. As the first week passed we made one or two more attempts to get back into our house. We watched mournfully through the window as Mrs Spick fed Tarquin strange inedible nosh that came in cubes, and Hoovered him as he ate.

But we couldn't get any closer because of the noxious vapours exuded by little box things labelled V-A-P-O-N-A, hung up in every room.

That house was so clean, it was toxic!

"It's a wonder they can breathe," I said to Nattie, as we flew despondently back to Bernie's for some proper food.

There was nothing for it but to resume our duties at Bernie's. But Bernie had got used to us being there, and after a while he stopped chasing us around, though we did our best to keep him going. Nattie even flew up his nose, which was above and beyond the call of duty, as I pointed out. But after eating, which was what he did most of the day, he would just lapse into a stupor in front of the TV, eventually falling asleep with his mouth open, so that we could pick the food out from between his teeth, and even crawl right in and jiggle his tonsils about.

Well, someone had to groom him.

From time to time Bernie made an effort to be friendly with the people next door, but it was no use. If Mrs Spick could have produced an enormous spray for him she would have done. He just had to stay on his side of the hedge and watch as Mrs Spick trimmed and shaved her garden. Within the week, no grass blade dared poke itself more than half an inch out of the ground, and even the insects formed an orderly row. Bernie stood at his front door watching, and from time to time offered unwelcome advice.

"I've got an old lawn mower you could use," he said. "Needs a bit of oil, but I could soon fix it up, right as rain."

Mrs Spick didn't even look up. "No

thank you," she said.

"You want to try a nice bit of manure on that," he said as she dug over a patch of ground near the hedge. "I know where you can get some."

"Your kitchen, no doubt," Mrs Spick said, but luckily Bernie didn't hear.

"Anything you need," he said, "Just let me know."

Mrs Spick stood up, looking at Bernie as though she might like to flush him down her toilet. "I don't suppose you could move your compost heap, could you?" she said, pointing to a messy heap of flowers, wood and old pram wheels propped up against their shared hedge. Bernie looked bewildered, then mildly outraged.

"That's my garden feature," he said.

Mrs Spick looked at him as though he'd just turned into a gorilla meringue.

"Well, it isn't finished yet," said Bernie, defensively.

Mrs Spick opened her mouth to say something, then changed her mind and went back inside, muttering to herself.

Once the garden was finally done, no one was allowed in it, not even Tarquin unless he wore specially protective clothing – an old boiler suit, rubber gloves, bike helmet and goggles. He had added a cape to this, in an attempt to look more like a superhero, and stood by himself in the middle of the lawn, not seeming to know what to do. Occasionally he looked up, and flapped his cape. Then, looking cautiously around for his mother, he dragged some of the planks that had been firmly pushed back into Bernie's side of the hedge into his own garden. He made a kind of ramp with them and ran up it, bouncing at the end before spreading his cape and leaping off.

Eventually I realised he was trying to fly. Copying the birds.

Birds! I thought. You won't get anywhere copying them. You can't learn about flying from birds. I mean, they're no good at it. They have to land sometime or they get tired and fall out of the air. And look at the way chicks just plummet out of the nest. Whereas us – we spend our entire lives in the air.

"About 330 times a second should do it," I buzzed in his ear as he flapped his cape again. But it was no good. After a while his mother called him and he had to dismantle his ramp and push it back through the hedge.

Once in a while we tried exercising him when his mother wasn't about, just to be friendly. But there was nothing friendly in the way he chased us, using an old tea towel like a whip. He was much *much* faster than Bernie.

Forward a bit – back – quick dart to the left – *ouch*!

I flapped off unsteadily to join Nattie in the safety of Bernie's garden. Tarquin's tea towel had grazed my back wing and leg.

"He winged me," I said in some astonishment. It's a disgrace for a fly ever to be winged by a human.

"Poor boy," Nattie sighed. "He's lonely."

"*Poor boy*?" I said, wondering if I could grow a new leg.

"Well she won't let the other children play with him," Nattie said. "And they all call him names. He's going to have a terrible time when school begins."

I glared over to where Tarquin stood, now flapping both his cape and the tea towel about. *Lonely*? I thought. Lonely is not a concept most flies understand.

"They're all lonely," Grandad said, as we joined him on some left-over gravy that was trickling down the kitchen units. "Even though they all live together, humans have the gift of loneliness," he said, lowering his proboscis into the gristly juice. "Not like us flies."

I suppose it's what happens when you

only lay one egg at a time. If you laid 2000 like us, you'd never be lonely.

Still, trying to exercise Tarquin was getting us nowhere, so we had to leave him and his mother to their own devices. And no sooner had we done that, than a quarrel blew up between Bernie and Mrs Spick.

First she complained about all the lovely, fatty, greasy smells wafting out of his kitchen window.

"Can you please keep your windows shut when you're cooking?" she asked him. "Tarquin's asthmatic."

Bernie stood with a piece of pizza clamped to the side of his face. He'd fallen asleep with his head in the box.

"I thought we might have a barbecue," he said. "Invite the little lad round."

"He's cleaning his room," said Mrs Spick.

"On a nice day like this?" said Bernie. "He should be out playing. Getting himself a bit grubby for a change."

Mrs Spick shuddered delicately, and turned to go.

"He wants some dirt under his fingernails," he called after her. "My old Nan used to say that every child should eat a pound of dirt when he's growing."

Mrs Spick looked at Bernie. Her gaze travelled slowly over his vest.

"I suppose that's what you had for breakfast," she said, and clicked her way up the path on her sharp little heels.

"Can't you clear some of this rubbish out of your garden?" she said, the next time she came out. "There'll be vermin."

So Bernie made a big bonfire and

started burning the rubbish. He lugged an old mattress on top of it and it blazed up so high it looked as though he might burn the house down. Great flakes of soot drifted over to Mrs Spick's washing. She ran out, coughing, into a cloud of filthy smoke to drag her washing back in, and a spark from Bernie's fire landed in the grass near her feet.

"Fire!" she screamed, very loudly and Bernie came running out with the water from his washing up bowl, that hadn't been changed in all the time we'd been there. Without hesitation, he flung it all over her.

Mrs Spick's face went quite blue. She just stood there, gasping and shuddering, bits of cold egg and porridge clinging to her hair.

"You – you health hazard!" she spluttered when she could finally speak. "I'll have the council on you!" and she ran back inside to sterilise all her clothes, and call the fire brigade. Bernie put the fire out with a very bad grace.

"Can't do right for doing wrong," he muttered, sending black looks across the hedge.

The next day, Mrs Spick was out again with her shears, clipping at the hedge while Bernie was out shopping. It took a long time.

PLEASE TIDY YOUR GARDEN, it read when she'd finished. Bernie came back and threw a fit. He banged on her door, leaving greasy smudges on the new paint, and when she came out there was a terrific row. Bernie's big deep voice and

83

her squeaky one could be heard right down the street. Eventually they both went in, slamming their doors, and Bernie's lounge window fell out.

"I told you humans can't get on," Grandad said, shaking his antennae. "When will they ever learn?"

None of this was helping us to get our house back. Whenever we approached Mrs Spick ran at us with the toxic spray and anything else that came to hand. I was beginning to think that maybe the idea of teaching humans to vomit all day long wasn't such a bad one. We wanted our house back.

"Maybe we should summon the whole clan," I said to Nattie. For while one or two flies don't seem like much of a challenge, 47 million of us can look quite impressive. But Nattie said we had to be patient.

"We've been patient for two million years," she said. "A few more days can't hurt. They'll adjust to us being here in the end."

So we went on trying to keep them company from a safe distance, and humming all our best tunes to cheer them up. But one day, as we flew around their door humming tunefully in an encouraging way, I heard Tarquin say to Mrs Spick, "I don't like it here, Mum."

"Never mind, Tarquin," Mrs Spick said. "If it gets too bad, we can always move."

"But Mum," Tarquin said sadly. "We've moved about twenty times already."

I looked at Nattie, and Nattie looked at

me. Our hums changed to a worried buzz.

The fact was that though Mrs Spick and Tarquin weren't exactly Friends of the Earth, or of any living creature that moved upon it, we didn't want them to move. The minute they moved out, all the spiders would move back in again. We could hear them holding their spidery conferences at night in the hedge at the bottom of the garden, which was the nearest they dared to go to the house, and weaving their wicked webs. Nattie and me certainly didn't want the spiders back. No. All we wanted was to live in peace in our own house again, taking care of our humans. It should have been simple, but it wasn't.

"There has to be something we can do," Nattie said.

Chapter Five
Flying machine

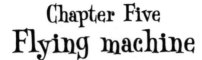

Now at the bottom of Bernie's garden, there was a shed. Not the one that was scattered across his garden, but a proper shed, painted green. He kept all his tools in it, and Bernie would disappear into that shed for hours at a time, when anything got him down, banging and sawing and drilling. He had been spending a lot of time in it recently since his window had fallen out. When

Mrs Spick complained about all the banging and hammering, he simply turned on his power drill, and the circular saw.

"He's just keeping himself busy," Nattie said.

Keeping himself busy – that's something humans are always trying to do. *Looking for something to do.* You won't catch insects looking for something to do – they always know what to do. But humans don't seem to know.

Anyway, the more Mrs Spick got at him, the more Bernie disappeared into his shed. The sounds of hammering and sawing filled his garden, the sounds of Hoovering and washing machines filled her house. Tarquin got fed up.

He had made his usual ramp and was

trying to run his remote control car up it. He was very proud of his remote control car, which had huge back wheels and flashing lights. It had worked perfectly when Mrs Spick had bought it for him a week ago, but now it only rolled backwards about a couple of centimetres, then stopped.

"I don't like it here," he whispered to a stray dandelion that had boldly poked its way under the hedge from Bernie's garden into Mrs Spick's. "There's nothing to do."

And he went back inside his house. There, unknown to Mrs Spick, who was busy ironing the Kleenex, he packed his wooden cart with useful things for his journey: a spare pair of shoes and wellies in case it rained, his pyjamas and toothbrush and dental floss, two teddies, a feather duster and the remote control car. Then he lowered the cart carefully down the stairs to the kitchen, and helped himself to some of Mrs Spick's Extra-Nutritious, Taste-Free bars, left a very neat note on the table for his mother, opened the back door and went out into the garden.

"What's he doing?" said Nattie in alarm.

"Running away, I think." I said. We looked at one another. Every fly knows that humans can't navigate. We buzzed round him anxiously as he pulled his cart along the garden path.

"You can't just run away," I buzzed. "You've got nowhere to go to."

"Your mum'll be worried," Nattie buzzed.

But humans have never been any good at listening to flies. All the wisdom, all the good advice, we've buzzed into your ears for millenia, and where has it got us?

Just like the rest of the human race Tarquin wasn't listening now. He pushed open the gate.

And at that moment, Bernie opened the door of his shed. He was covered in wood shavings. He looked down at Tarquin.

"What are you doing?" he said, then his eyes narrowed suspiciously. "Has your mum sent you?"

"No," Tarquin said. "I'm running away."

"Running away?" Bernie said. His gaze travelled over Tarquin's boiler suit, rubber gloves, bike helmet, cape and goggles.

"You don't think you might be a bit noticeable in that outfit?" he said.

Tarquin hung his head. From his house came the sound of the vacuum cleaner, whirring into action. Bernie rolled his eyes.

"Too clean for you is it," he said, sympathetically, but Tarquin shook his head.

"No," he said, "It's just – there's nothing to do."

Bernie's gaze lighted on the cart. "Is that a remote control car?" he asked suddenly.

Tarquin nodded. "But it doesn't work," he said, sadly.

"Can I see it? – No, tell you what – bring it in here."

Tarquin hesitated. I could practically hear his mother's voice in his head, telling him that he was in no circumstances to set foot on Bernie's property. But, well, he wasn't supposed to run away either.

"Come on, lad," Bernie said, waving him in. Tarquin pulled his cart through the gate.

Bernie's shed was a revelation. That shed was immaculate! Screws gleamed, screw drivers and hammers hung from special hooks in the walls. Everything was labelled and in its place. Old Coathangers, one box said, and Corkscrews, said another. Screws, nails, nuts and bolts, each had different cartons and all of them shone as if they'd been newly polished. Me and Nattie flew round the shelves to investigate. There was nothing for a fly to recycle at all – no dust, no oil.

Tarquin blinked.

A work bench took up most of the shed floor, and on top of it was a large wooden frame, held together with what looked like toilet paper, coathangers, cotton bobbins, and lollipop sticks. There was a bit of dust, and some wood shavings scattered around this, but it was very clean dust.

"What is it?" Tarquin, Nattie and me all asked.

"It's a little project I've been working on," said Bernie. He picked it up.

"There," he said proudly. "What do you think about that?"

"Er," said Tarquin.

"It's a glider," said Bernie. As soon as he said it, we could all see that it was. It had a wing span of about one metre, a little rudder, and a propellor.

Tarquin's face lit up.

"A flying machine!" he said, then, "But will it fly?"

"Well now," Bernie said. "That's where your remote control might come in handy."

Tarquin's face fell. "But it doesn't work," he said. "I've changed the batteries and everything."

"Don't you worry about that," Bernie said. "Hand it over."

For the rest of that morning Tarquin and Bernie worked on the glider, spraying the tissues, tuning the radio receiver, adjusting the nose to tail ratio, fastening the skid on with pegs.

Bernie was a different man in his shed.

"Rudder to the vertical tail fin," he said.

"Elevator to the horizontals."

"Aileron to the wing flaps for lateral control."

"Actuators on."

Tarquin passed him the tools he needed, the screw driver, scalpel, pliers and tiny chisel, and attached little lead weights to the nose and tail with Blutac.

Finally they sprayed the whole thing with a special waterproof paint.

"There we are," said Bernie at last. "What do you want to call it?"

Tarquin's face was pink with excitement, instead of its usual pale green.

"Can we call it 'Tarquin'?" he said.

"Course we can!" said Bernie, and he let Tarquin paint his name on it – Tarquin 1. It took a long time, because he was very careful not to let the letters wobble.

All this time I had been finding the whole job almost as fascinating as Tarquin did. I buzzed in and out of the cockpit, and landed on the tail fin, carefully, so as not to smudge the paint.

"You can move the rudder backwards and forwards," I called to Nattie. "And the propellor spins round and round!"

But Nattie was flitting from side to side, in the way that she does when she's nervous. I landed beside her on the shelf.

"What is it, Nattie?" I asked.

"Why does Bernie want a flying machine?" she said. I looked at her blankly.

"Everyone wants to fly," I said, but Nattie shook her antennae.

"Remember what Grandad said," she replied, and I looked even more blank. What had Grandad said about humans making flying machines?

That they only used them for war.

But Tarquin and Bernie had never looked so happy. They were working together in harmony, thoroughly absorbed. Bernie was even buzzing, but not any tune we knew.

"Surely not," I said, but Nattie said, "We have to warn Mrs Spick. We have to at least let her know where Tarquin is, or there will be a war."

She had a point there. "OK," I said cautiously. Mrs Spick, if you remember, won't let a fly within three metres of her home. "But how?"

Nattie buzzed impatiently round in a little spiral.

"Leave it to me," she said.

Chapter Six
One small step

Meanwhile Mrs Spick was busy
Hoovering the individual pages of
Tarquin's books. She was humming too,
a perky little song about vacuum cleaner
accessories. She seemed happy and
absorbed, though not too distracted to
forget the toxic spray, which she fished
out of her pocket as soon as we
appeared. Luckily we were ready for
her this time.

"Quick!" cried Nattie, flying in great zig-zags across the room. We flew ahead of Mrs Spick, all the way down the stairs to the kitchen, and landed on the note.

"Look – look!" Nattie cried, and I crawled around the outline of the writing.

Dear Mum, I am running away, it read. *Love Tarquin.*

Mrs Spick paused, with the toxic spray held aloft. We ascended gracefully as she read Tarquin's note, and watched with interest as she turned as pale as the paper it was written on. She sat down heavily. "Tarquin," she whispered.

"He's with Bernie!" we buzzed right in her face, but it was as though she could neither hear nor see. Then she got up and was soon running in and out of all the rooms of the house, the front garden and then the back.

"Tarquin, Tarquin, Tarquin!" she screeched, just like some strange bird.

"He's in Bernie's shed!" Nattie and I buzzed round her, but she took no notice.

She opened the garden gate and ran up and down the lane, shouting for Tarquin, but Bernie had switched the circular saw on again in the shed, and there was so much noise that they didn't hear. Mrs Spick ran back to the house. She was rapidly becoming hysterical. Neither me nor Nattie knew what to do. If she phoned the police, they might arrest Bernie. Then there would be a war.

"We've got to show her where he is," Nattie buzzed.

"But how?" I buzzed back.

"We've got to distract her," she said, and without thinking I flew straight at Mrs Spick with my loudest buzz.

Even in the midst of her distress Mrs Spick hadn't forgotten the toxic spray. Blasted full on by a jet of choking fumes, I spiralled downwards, out of control.

"Kiko, Kiko!" Nattie cried.

Stunned, I lay on my back on the carpet, all my legs twitching convulsively. Nattie's hum rose to its highest pitch ever.

"You *silly* woman!" she shrilled, and flew straight up Mrs Spick's nose.

Pandemonium erupted.

Mrs Spick flew round her kitchen, batting wildly at her own face. I flapped my wings feebly once, twice and rose, tilting dangerously into the air. With each whirring beat of my wings I felt stronger.

Flight is beauty, flight is joy, I hummed, drunkenly and –

If you want to be a fly, fly, fly,

Then you have to try, try, try.

Unfortunately, out of control of my flight path, I buzzed straight into Mrs Spick, butting her in the face. She shot out of the house, screaming.

Time for me to lead her straight up the garden path.

She could move fast, Mrs Spick, but fortunately no human moves as fast as a fly. Our reflexes are five times faster than yours and urrrrgh! A great splot of fly spray caught my rear end just as I flew over the hedge. With my last effort

I butted into the door of Bernie's shed. Mrs Spick sprinted after me, then stopped. She looked round, clutching her face, as though the agony of realising that she might never see him again had only just hit her.

"TAAARQUIINN!" she screamed.

Tarquin opened the door of the shed.

"Yes Mum?" he asked.

I sank down onto a leaf feeling gutted and sick. Mrs Spick clutched Tarquin crying, "Oh thank goodness, oh, I thought I'd never see you again." And similar phrases. I felt too sick and dizzy to move. Nattie emerged rather stickily from Mrs Spick's nose and landed beside me.

"Kiko," she said. "Are you all right?"

"I will be," I said. Each panel of my eyes was showing me a different scene, which was terribly confusing. Rather like watching a hundred televisions at once.

Meanwhile Mrs Spick was saying, "What are you doing here, in this dirty, horrible shed?"

Then she looked up, and gasped. For the shed was spotless. She couldn't have cleaned it better herself. And Bernie was just sweeping up the last of the wood shavings. He beamed at Mrs Spick.

"Look what Tarquin's made," he said, and proudly Tarquin held out his magnificent flying machine.

Mrs Spick blinked, as if she couldn't believe her eyes. She held out her hands, which were trembling, and gently Tarquin placed the brand new glider into them. She held it reverently.

"Oh – it's beautiful," she gasped.

Suddenly she looked quite emotional. "When I was a little girl, all I ever wanted to be was a pilot," she said. "Just like Amy Johnson. But my mum said I had to start work at the cleaning agency."

"Come and watch it fly, mum," Tarquin said.

Together, the three of them went into the garden. Bernie raised Tarquin onto his greasy shoulders, despite a murmur of protest from Mrs Spick, and Tarquin launched the glider. It whirred into activity and flew! And flew, and flew! The remote control steered the rudder, and Tarquin directed it all the way back to the garden path. Even me and Nattie were impressed.

"Lad's a natural," Bernie said. "But he was on his way out of the garden when

I found him. Said he was running away."

Mrs Spick put her hand on Bernie's arm. And she wasn't even wearing her rubber gloves.

"I can't thank you enough," she said.

Nattie looked at me. I looked at Nattie. "Grandad has to see this," she said. Buzzing with excitement, we flew back to the house.

"Grandad! Grandad!" we cried. "Come and watch this!"

We paused in mid air, because the house seemed quite empty. Then Grandad emerged like a scuba diver from a pan full of cold baked beans. He looked at us vaguely and we could tell he was searching his memory annals again.

"It's Kiko!" I told him, to save time.

"And Nattie," Nattie put in.

"Tarquin and Bernie are friends!" we cried together.

"What?" Grandad said. "Never!"

"It's true!" we told him. "They've made a flying machine!"

Grandad nearly toppled back into the baked beans. He gazed at us in astonishment, then flew with us out of the window. Together the three of us watched the three of them, happily taking turns with the remote control.

"I don't believe it," Grandad said.

We watched as they learned how to make the glider do the loop, the dive, the slow roll, the pin roll, the inverted spin, the bunt, the pinwheel, and even an arabesque.

"Well, who would have thought it?" said Grandad. We could see him encoding additional annotations to the Flyrule in his memory annals: *Flying can bring humans together.* And it was true.

Soon Tarquin, Bernie and Mrs Spick were surrounded by children from the estate, all of whom wanted a go.

"Well, it's Tarquin's plane," said Bernie. Tarquin hesitated, then he smiled and held out the plane to the nearest boy, whose face lit up. Soon they were all taking turns with the glider, making it spin and dip, and fly on its back. Young and old, scruffy and neat – everyone was cheering and clapping, brought together by the magic of flight.

"That's one small step for mankind," said Grandad.

Finally Bernie, Tarquin and Mrs Spick had had enough. We followed them back towards Tarquin's house, where, already, the beautiful dust was settling.

"Can I make more planes, mum?" Tarquin asked.

"He's welcome round at my place, any time," Bernie said.

Mrs Spick stopped short. "*Your* place?" she said. If she'd had any antennae, they would have been quivering.

"Oh can I Mum, can I?" said Tarquin.

"Not in that house," she said. "It'll trigger your allergies. You can work in the shed."

"Well," said Bernie, "If we're building bigger planes, we might need to do some of the work in the house. I don't suppose you'd want all the dirt and mess round at yours."

Mrs Spick thought hard. "You could always clean your house," she said.

This was a whole new concept for Bernie. There are a hundred billion neurons in the human brain, and you could see them all struggling to make a connection.

"Clean – the – house?" he said, very slowly.

"How is it," Mrs Spick said, "that you can keep your shed spotless, but your house is like a council tip?"

"Clean – the – house?" Bernie said again. Mrs Spick sighed.

"I tell you what," she said. "You can teach both me and Tarquin to build planes – I'll teach you to clean your house."

"Clean –"

"Yes." Mrs Spick interrupted firmly. "In fact, we'll start now. Tarquin – fetch the rubber gloves. And the hose."

Mrs Spick made them put on masks, caps, aprons and wellies. Bravely they squelched across the carpet in the hall. That was the only bit of carpet they could stand on, since the rest of it was covered with crockery, magazines, tools and bits of car. Fearless as Mrs Spick was when it came to cleaning, she flinched when she saw the kitchen.

"Right," she said. "Open all the windows. Tarquin – fetch the wheelbarrow, two gallons of bleach, one gallon of vinegar, the industrial strength ammonia, two pounds of rock salt, fourteen lemons and a hairnet."

Tarquin scampered off.

For the next few hours, Mrs Spick, Bernie and Tarquin were busy as bees. Or flies, since bees are nowhere *near* as busy as flies. Bernie and Tarquin ran back and forth to the wheelie bins, Mrs Spick attacked all the surfaces with lemons, ammonia and bleach. Grandad got quite worried in case she managed to turn Bernie's house into a fly-free zone like hers, but there didn't seem much danger of that, since some of the dirt had been ingrained for decades. However, slowly but surely it did start to resemble a human home.

Bernie got quite emotional when they found the living-room carpet.

"Oh, it's red," he said. "My old mum always told me it was!"

Finally, as evening gathered, Bernie's house looked transformed. You could actually see through the windows, and there was room to sit down. Mrs Spick made them all a cup of tea in the newly-bleached mugs, and they all sank down, exhausted.

"Now," she said. "I hope you're going to keep up with this. I'll be checking on you. No more fish and chips in the bath – no more oiling wheels on the cooker!"

Bernie looked abashed. "No, Mrs Spick."

Mrs Spick patted his arm. "You can call me Doreen," she said.

From that time on, there were no more arguments between Bernie and Mrs Spick. She made sure he cleaned his house once every week, he showed her how to build planes. Doreen got so interested in the principles of aerodynamics that sometimes she forgot to wash up, and there was plenty of half-finished food left in her kitchen. Tarquin became something of an expert on flight. By the time he went to school, he already knew the other children and they all wanted to play in his home. With all this extra activity going on, his house became ever-so-slightly messy – just grubby enough for us flies to live there in peace, and help with the recycling.

It was as though they had all evolved.

Chapter Seven
Agents of human destiny

"Grandad," Nattie said. "What about the Flyrule?"

"Hummm – whassat?" Grandad said. He had just flown in on the glider, clinging with his sticky feet to the underside of one of the wings.

"The Flyrule,"Nattie said. "You said it hasn't been changed for centuries."

"'S'right," said Grandad, performing a beautiful spiral twist before landing on the window sill.

"Well," said Nattie. "Look at them!"

We all looked at Bernie, Tarquin and Mrs Spick, playing happily together in the evening light. Grandad beamed with joy. "Yes, look at them," he said. "It does my old thorax good. I never thought I'd see the day. It's almost as it – as if – "

"They've evolved!" said Nattie, and all three of us looked at one another, our six hundred eye panels glowing in the light from the setting sun.

"It's time, Grandad," Nattie said, and Grandad looked quite overcome.

"Oh but," he said, and "You don't mean – " then, "Well I...I don't see why not!" and he looked at us in astonished wonder. "Yes!" he said. "Why not? All flies everywhere should know about this!

We will – we'll put it in the Flyrule!"

"Hurrah!" cried me and Nattie. Then the three of us settled on the cooker to take a bit of sustenance first, because this was going to be a long job.

Finally we formed a circle. Grandad filled both his thorax and abdomen with air and we did the same. Then he began to hum, on a special frequency quite out of the range of human ears. As we joined in with him it felt as though we were spiralling backwards through thousands of years, and ages of evolution – all the way back to that moment when the very first human stood on his hind legs and the Flyrule began. Higher and higher his hum rose, into the encoding frequency that every fly knows. We could feel the whole of our bodies vibrating with it, and we knew that simultaneously the message was passing from one fly to another all over the world, from Greenland to Japan, India to Russia, the North to the South Pole, like an electric charge.

And this is what it said:

IMPORTANT NOTICE:
Flying can bring people together
and
Co-operation is the key
to human evolution

Well!

The news caused a sensation all over the world. Thousands of flies flew in from Alaska and Indonesia and Tunbridge Wells, just to see Bernie,

Tarquin and Mrs Spick frolicking in the garden. And they were so absorbed in what they were doing that they didn't even notice!

Grandad became famous and was asked over and over again to tell his story.

"Don't ask me," he kept saying. "It's not my story – ask Meano and Tattie!"

And so they did – so many times that eventually we decided to encode it into the fly's memory annals to save time. It has its own special section so that flies of the future will always be able to learn from it, just as you're learning now – *Section 4619832 HOW TO EVOLVE YOUR HUMAN IN SIX EASY STAGES* by Kiko and Nattie.

Agents of human destiny – that's us!

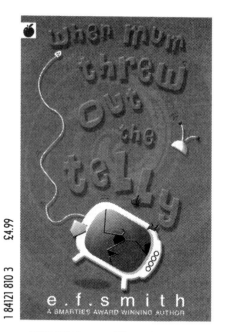

1 84121 810 3   £4.99

EMILY SMITH

Jeff really liked television. Cartoons were more interesting than life. Sit-coms were funnier than life. And in life you never got to watch someone trying to ride a bike over an open sewer. Sometimes at night Jeff even dreamed television. Mum complained, but it didn't make any difference. Jeff didn't take any notice of her, which was a mistake.

A very funny and thought-provoking book from Emily Smith, winner of two Smarties Prizes.

£4.99

1 84121 456 6

PAT MOON

Loads of secret stuff about BOYS, worry bugs,
babies, enemies, etcetera, etcetera.
Snoopers will be savaged by Twinkle
(warrior-princess guinea pig).

Also by Pat Moon:
Do Not Read This Book was shortlisted
for the Sheffield Book Award

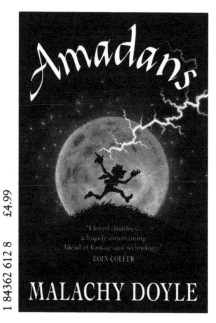

MALACHY DOYLE

'I've had enough of these Amadans, trying to scare everyone,' said Jimmy. 'I think it's about time we found out who they are and what they're up to.'

Enter the fantastical world of the Amadans in this enthralling read.

'I loved *Amadans*...a hugely entertaining blend of fantasy and technology.'
Eoin Colfer

MICHAEL LAWRENCE

The underpants from hell – that's what
Jiggy calls them, and not just because they look so gross.
No, these pants are evil.
And they're in control. Of him. Of his life!
Can Jiggy get to the bottom of his
problem before it's too late?

"...the funniest book I've ever read."
Teen Titles

"Hilarious!"
The Independent

Winner of the Stockton Children's
Book of the Year Award

RED APPLES FROM ORCHARD

JIGGY McCUE STORIES by MICHAEL LAWRENCE

DO NOT READ . . . by PAT MOON

JAMIE B STORIES by CERI WORMAN

Red Apple books are available from all good bookshops, or can be ordered direct from the publisher:
Orchard Books, PO Box 29, Douglas, IM99 1BQ.
Credit card orders please telephone 01624 836000 or fax 01624 837033 or email:
bookshop@enterprise.net for details.

To order please quote title, author and ISBN and your full name and address. Cheques and postal
orders should be made payable to 'Bookpost plc'. Postage and packing is FREE within the UK
(overseas customers should add £1.00 per book).

Prices and availability are subject to change.

About the author

Livi Michael lives near Manchester, with two sons and a dog. She has written six books for children, including the series of books about Frank the hamster, which was shortlisted for the Branford Boase prize, and *The Whispering Road*, shortlisted for the Ottaker's Book Award. Livi spends most of her time at her kitchen table with her lap top, where, all last summer, she was accompanied by two flies. Eventually she gave up the fruitless task of trying to get rid of them, and decided to find out more about them instead.

ORCHARD BOOKS
96 Leonard Street, London EC2A 4XD
Orchard Books Australia, Hachette Children's Books
Level 17/207 Kent Street, Sydney, NSW 2000
A Paperback Original
First published in Great Britain in 2005
Text © copyright Livi Michael 2005
The right of Livi Michael to be identified as the author
of this work has been asserted by her in accordance with
the Copyright, Designs and Patents Act, 1988.

A CIP catalogue record for this book
is available from the British Library.
ISBN 1 84362 725 6
1 3 5 7 9 10 8 6 4 2
Printed in Great Britain